SOMETHING SLIMY ON PRIMROSE DRIVE

Black Cats

The Ramsbottom Rumble • Georgia Byng
Calamity Kate • Terry Deary
The Custard Kid • Terry Deary
The Ghosts of Batwing Castle • Terry Deary
Ghost Town • Terry Deary
Into the Lion's Den • Terry Deary
The Joke Factory • Terry Deary
The Treasure of Crazy Horse • Terry Deary
The Wishing Well Ghost • Terry Deary
A Witch in Time • Terry Deary
Dear Ms • Joan Poulson
It's a Tough Life • Jeremy Strong
Big Iggy • Kaye Umansky
Something Slimy on Primrose Drive • Karen Wallace

First published 2002 by
A & C Black Publishers Ltd
37 Soho Square, London W1D 3QZ
www.acblack.com

ISBN 0-7136-5993-9

A CIP catalogue for this book is available from the British Library.

A & C Black uses paper produced with elemental
chlorine-free pulp, harvested from managed sustainable forests.

Printed and bound in Spain by G. Z. Printek, Bilbao.

SOMETHING SLIMY ON PRIMROSE DRIVE

KAREN WALLACE

ILLUSTRATED BY
HELEN FLOOK

A & C BLACK • LONDON

Hilary D. with thanks
K.W.

Chapter One

Primrose Drive was the sort of street where neat, tidy people lived neat, tidy lives.

Every house shone with new paint. Every flowerbed was criss-crossed with rows of brightly-coloured flowers. And the lawns around them were so beautifully mown, the grass looked as if it was made of plastic.

Beside every house on Primrose Drive was a brand-new car that was always washed, brushed and polished on Saturdays.

For every car there was a garage that was stocked with the latest DIY equipment. Of course, most of the tools were still in their boxes. This was because the men on Primrose Drive only compared their drills and power saws. They never used them.

After all, the men on Primrose Drive knew that DIY was a messy business. Worse, their wives knew that some of those oily stains were impossible to clean. No matter how long you soaked them.

And that was exactly the sort of thing that mattered to the women on Primrose Drive because they liked things as neat and tidy as their husbands. Indeed, when the people on Primrose Drive asked each other over for supper, nobody was interested in the food. All they wanted to see was a clean and tidy house and their reflection in really shiny silver candlesticks. They didn't care about tasty casseroles or yummy puddings. All they wanted to smell was furniture polish. As for children on Primrose Drive, there were hardly any. Everyone agreed children were noisy and messy. No matter what you did they were always heard and it was impossible not to see them.

So it was not surprising that the neat and tidy people of Primrose Drive were fast asleep when two coal-black horses pulling a huge old-fashioned carriage, clip-clopped down the street on the dot of midnight.

It was a strange-looking carriage. Not only because it had four creaky spider-web wheels and was loaded with what looked like coffins and hat boxes. The carriage also looked peculiar because it was covered in tendrils of dripping scum and water-weed. It looked as if it had been driven through a swamp at high speed. Which is exactly what had happened, since Boris Wolfbane liked going fast and the Wolfbanes' last home had been in a swamp.

As for the timing of their arrival on Primrose Drive, Boris and his wife Anaconda had decided to take this very seriously. So they had gone with their children Clod and Pearl to consult the sacred bonfire of some thousand-year-old rubbish.

In the stinking grey curls of smoke, the message had been clear:

Move at midnight.

It will bring peace and prosperity.

And it won't disturb the neighbours.

Because more than anything else, Boris and Anaconda Wolfbane were anxious to make a good impression on their neighbours. Especially now that Pearl and Clod were getting older, Anaconda and Boris wanted them to have the kind of childhood they had heard about on the radio or seen through windows on other people's televisions.

And No. 34 Primrose Drive seemed the ideal place to begin.

****

Inside the slimy black carriage, Anaconda wrapped up the leftovers of their picnic supper – chilled toadburgers with all the trimmings.

She sighed. Nowadays, there were always leftovers because Pearl Wolfbane refused to eat what her mother cooked.

Anaconda patted Pearl's cheek with her long silvery fingers. 'I wish you'd try a little bit of toadburger,' she said. 'It tastes just like chicken, you know.'

'I know, Mum,' replied Pearl Wolfbane kindly. She leant back into the buttoned velvet seat. 'But I'd rather eat chicken like everyone else.'

Anaconda put a cold damp hand on her daughter's forehead. It was warm and dry. Maybe she was sickening for something.

'I'll make green stew with grey lumps for our first breakfast,' said Anaconda quickly. 'You used to love that.'

'I like green stew!' Clod Wolfbane nudged his sister. In the light of the moon, Pearl could see his purple eyes shining. 'Come on, Pearl, you know green stew makes really good glue when it's cold.'

Anaconda patted her son's matted black hair. 'You say the sweetest things, Clod,' she murmured.

At that moment, the carriage stopped and Boris Wolfbane's head appeared upside down at the window.

Anaconda could hardly stop herself clapping her hands with delight. After all these years, Boris was still so wonderfully bat-like!

'We're here!' cried Boris in a voice that sounded like a rock rattling around on a drum. Clod and Pearl scrambled out of their seats and jumped to the ground. Anaconda oozed out of the door like a stream of mercury.

For a moment nobody spoke. Pearl was staring so hard she thought her eyes might pop out.

She was standing in a cul-de-sac. In front of her was a perfectly ordinary house. Beside it was another perfectly ordinary house. Bright new paint gleamed in the moonlight. Flowerbeds circled lawns so beautifully mown, the grass looked like plastic. There was even a garage and a place to park a car.

'Which one is ours?' whispered Pearl. She was so happy she could barely speak.

Boris Wolfbane flipped backwards and spread his cloak so that he fluttered gently to the ground in front of No. 34.

Pearl hugged herself with joy. She had never

seen such a lovely house. It was exquisitely, amazingly, unbelievably normal.

Clod Wolfbane turned to his sister and rolled his eyes. 'Wow!' he whispered. 'Weird or what?'

Chapter Two

The next morning Anaconda Wolfbane tied on her favourite apron – the yellow one with black markings – and ladled out four bowls of green stew with grey lumps in it.

Anaconda was very excited. During the night, once the children were asleep, she and Boris had worked on converting the kitchen using a digger that had silently and mysteriously appeared. Anaconda wanted to do everything she could to make Clod and Pearl feel completely at home for their first breakfast.

Of course, Boris had teased Anaconda and called her new kitchen a glorified cave. But Anaconda didn't mind a bit. She knew her kitchen wasn't a cave. It was an open-plan subterranean space with mud effects on the ceiling.

As for the film of water that ran down the walls, Anaconda had chosen the colour specially. It was a tangy burnt orange. Not at all the sort of thing you would find in a cave!

'More stew, dear?' asked Anaconda as Clod slurped up the last chewy mouthful.

Clod nodded and pushed his bowl forward.

'Pearl?'

'No thanks, Mum,' replied Pearl. 'I had some Weetabix and yoghurt earlier.'

'Yuck,' muttered Clod. 'That sounds disgusting!'

'Now, Clod,' said Boris as he picked his teeth with a chicken bone. 'We all choose to express ourselves in different ways.'

Anaconda smiled to herself. Boris must have been reading her *Happy Families Handbook*. It said that sort of thing on every page.

Boris put down his bone and a broad grin spread across his face.

'And talking about expressing ourselves,' he laughed. 'Have you seen my brand-new swimming pool?'

Pearl's pale round face lit up with delight. A swimming pool! Pearl had read about swimming pools in *Felicity – A Happy Girl's Story*. In the book, Felicity's father had surprised his family with a wonderful swimming pool. It had shell-shaped tiles around the edge and the inside was painted blue so that the water sparkled in the sun. At one end, there was a changing hut that looked like a doll's house. The whole thing was surrounded by a low wall and flowering bushes.

But for Pearl, the best bits of all were the parties and barbecues Felicity threw for her friends. Everyone loved swimming and soon Felicity had become the most popular girl in the neighbourhood.

Pearl's blue eyes shone like sapphires.

'Oh, Dad!' she cried. 'I've always wanted a

swimming pool. Now we can have parties and barbecues!'

Certainly Boris was rather pleased with himself. He, too, had discovered that swimming pools went very well with crowds and roasting flesh, and generally getting to know people.

So while Anaconda put the final touches to her kitchen, Boris had busied himself in the garden. What's more, everything had been so quick and easy! After he'd laid the dynamite charges, all Boris had to do was stand back and push the plunger.

BOOM! What had been a lawn became a huge ragged crater! And best of all, it had filled to the top with muddy brown water. Exactly as Boris had planned!

Clod was so excited, he swallowed the last grey lump in one. 'Can we see your pool, Dad?' he cried, choking and shouting at once.

'Of course you can,' replied Boris proudly. 'I've even put a few snakes in it to make it look prettier.'

'Snakes?' said Pearl in a puzzled voice. As she spoke a tiny suspicion began to spread like a pool of syrup in her mind.

Maybe Boris's swimming pool wasn't like the one in *Felicity – A Happy Girl's Story*, after all.

'And toads and frogs and a few lizards,' continued Boris happily.

The pool of suspicion in Pearl's mind turned into a lake.

'I love swimming with snakes,' cried Anaconda. 'They're so friendly.'

'Especially when they wrap themselves around your legs,' cried Clod.

Anaconda clapped her hands with delight.

'That's a good idea, darling! Let's have a dip!'

'Last one in's a sissy!' whooped Clod.

There was a screech of wooden stools against rock floors. And suddenly Anaconda, Boris and Clod were all gone and Pearl was left in the kitchen alone.

Pearl stood up and touched the orange-coloured water that poured down the walls. It was cool and felt faintly refreshing when she patted a few drops on her forehead.

Pearl didn't really mind having a water hole crawling with snakes instead of a swimming pool. In a way, it would be more of a surprise if it was anything different. It was just that Pearl wished her family would do *something* that was the same as other people. Or at least a bit the same.

Pearl walked up the spiral stone stairs and pushed aside the thick mat of hanging vines that was the door. And just as she had expected, where only yesterday there had been a perfectly mown lawn, she found herself looking at a ragged mud hole full of water.

Pearl watched as her mother and brother splashed and played one of their favourite games in the bright green algae floating on the surface. Clod swam as fast as he could and made a path through the scum. Then at the count of ten Anaconda had to catch him before the scum closed over the water again.

'Whaddyathink?' cried Boris, as he leaned forward to dive in from an overhanging branch.

'It's brilliant, Dad,' called Pearl in the most enthusiastic voice she could manage.

SPLOT!

Boris dropped into the middle of the pond.

'I knew you'd like it,' he spluttered as he surfaced in the water.

It's brilliant Dad

At that moment, Clod paddled towards them. A large green frog was sitting on his head.

'Mum says we can do what we like with our bedrooms,' he shouted to his sister. 'She says I can have my scorpions and everything!'

'Of course you can, darling,' said Anaconda. She chortled happily as a thick black and yellow snake slid through the water in front of her face. 'We must all be allowed to express our feelings in the things we choose to surround ourselves with.'

Anaconda felt very proud of herself. She had remembered almost perfectly the top paragraph of Page 2 of *The Happy Families Handbook*.

Boris hauled himself out of the pond and sat on the edge where Pearl was standing.

Sunlight sparkled in Pearl's long, blonde hair. Her Cupid's bow mouth was pink as a rosebud against her creamy skin. Boris never tired of looking at his daughter. She was so pale and golden and beautiful. So completely and utterly different from the rest of her family.

'Have you thought how you'd like your bedroom, Pearl?' asked Boris kindly.

Pearl sat down and wound her fingers through her father's hand.

'Yes,' she said. 'I've thought about it a lot.'

In fact Pearl had thought about nothing else all those times when she had stared at bedroom walls hollowed out of vast tree trunks or cut from sheer rock or hung with seaweed or animal skins or covered in woven feathers.

And the thought had always started off the same way. 'When I get my own bedroom...'

'My room is going to be pink and white,' said Pearl firmly. 'I shall have wallpaper with ribbons and flowers on it, teddy bears on my bed and a dressing table with a lacy frill around it.'

For a second nobody spoke.

Then a large bubble went POP! as Anaconda's head sank beneath the scum.

Chapter Three

The Wolfbanes weren't the only family to arrive in Primrose Drive at midnight.

A few days later, another family, the Rigid-Smythes, drove towards Primrose Drive in their brand-new, silver estate car. Pamela and Dudley, with their two children Simon and Ruby, were coming home from their annual holiday abroad.

Not that the Rigid-Smythes usually travelled at midnight. In this case, their late arrival was entirely due to their plane being delayed. A completely unavoidable event that Pamela and Dudley Rigid-Smythe were none too pleased about.

Pamela was particularly cross because she had made a special light supper and put it in the freezer. Of course, the vegetable crumble could be eaten at any time but Pamela had dated it and stacked it so it would be easy to find on their first night back and she didn't like unexpected changes in her arrangements.

Dudley Rigid-Smythe was cross, too.

He had arranged to play a very important game of golf the next morning, with a business associate called Sid Bouncer.

Dudley had met Sid at the golf club a couple of months ago and had taken a liking to him immediately. Sid was clever at business and a man of the world like himself. What's more Sid had come up with a money-making proposition that interested Dudley very much indeed.

Sid had suggested that they should buy the empty house beside Dudley's, that is to say No. 34 Primrose Drive, split it into flats and sell them at a huge profit. Sid had a contact in the Mayor's office so there'd be no problem with planning permission. He would organize the builders and oversee the work. All Dudley had to do was come up with half of the money in cash.

In the beginning Dudley was a bit nervous about this. The only cash he had was in a savings account earmarked for Ruby and Simon. But then Sid had explained how every clever businessman had to speculate in order to accumulate.

Dudley blushed in the darkness of his car. At first he hadn't understood exactly what that meant. Then Sid explained it another way. A clever businessman has to take risks in order to make lots of money. If you play things safe all your life, you will never be a millionaire.

And Dudley wanted to be a millionaire more than anything else in the whole, wide world. Even though his family were already comfortably off and could afford anything they wanted.

Dudley was sure that if he was a millionaire, people would take more notice of him.

Now as Dudley drove through the midnight hour he got crosser and crosser. Not only would he lose his full eight hours sleep (which always made him cranky), he would also lose the advantage of his holiday where he had spent all day, every day practising his golf swing and whacking golf balls into a net.

Because even though he and Sid were business partners and they had met at the golf club, Dudley and Sid had never actually played one another. Now Dudley really wanted to beat Sid at their first game. In Dudley's book beating people was the only way to impress them.

In the back seat of the brand-new estate car, Simon Rigid-Smythe let himself fall into a light doze. He didn't mind what time he got home as long as he could start wearing lots of clothes again. Every morning for the past two weeks, he had been forced to listen to his mother moan on about how pale and skinny he looked in his swimming trunks. How he was delicate just like her great-uncle George. How he should take better care of himself. Eat healthy food. Play beach football with the other boys.

Poor Simon. Eventually he had taken to wearing a dressing-gown in the sea. He told his mother he was protecting himself from the sun.

Beside Simon his sister, Ruby, stared into the night. Ruby loved being up late. She loved everything to do with the night – its deep velvety blackness, its silvery glow, its long mysterious shadows. But best of all, Ruby loved staring into a full moon. Especially a full moon at midnight.

At that moment Ruby saw a cloud turn itself into a dragon. 'Mum!' cried Ruby. 'There's a dragon flying across the moon!'

'Shh! Ruby,' replied Pamela sternly. 'You'll wake your brother.'

'I'm awake,' muttered Simon quickly.

As he spoke he looked up at the moon. The dragon cloud was still there!

'I can see it, too!' cried Simon. 'Mum! Look! It's amazing!'

But when Mrs Rigid-Smythe looked, all she saw was a round moon with wispy shadows across it.

'I've never heard such rubbish,' muttered Pamela. She turned and glared at her daughter. 'How many times do I have to tell you? STOP making up stories.'

'Now, now, Pamela,' muttered Dudley as he gripped the wheel of his car with his new summer-weight driving gloves. When his wife got cross, Dudley made a big effort to appear reasonable.

'We've had a nice holiday. We're all tired. I'm sure Ruby and Simon were only imagining things.'

'I wasn't imagining anything,' muttered Ruby. 'I saw a dragon.'

Dudley Rigid-Smythe ignored his daughter and laughed a short bark of a laugh. 'Anyway, in five minutes, I imagine we'll all be in our beds.'

Pamela Rigid-Smythe sighed. She hadn't meant to be so sharp with Ruby, but she wished her daughter could be like other girls. Pamela's mouth turned into a thin, hard line.

For the past two weeks, she had tried everything to get Ruby to join in with the other families on the beach. After all there were lots of girls her age to play with. There were even discos to go to and a wonderful shopping centre only a few minutes' walk away. But Ruby didn't like discos and she hated shopping. So while all the other girls twittered and twirled or tried on clothes, Ruby sat by herself staring into an enormous rock pool.

Mrs Rigid-Smythe shivered in the darkness of the car. One day she had seen Ruby dangling her hand in the rock pool. There were baby octopuses wrapped round her fingers like rings! It was absolutely disgusting.

The car filled with a thick, bad-tempered silence as Dudley turned into Primrose Drive and drove past the tidy flowerbeds and beautifully mown lawns towards their house at the end of the cul-de-sac.

'Almost ho—,' he said brightly. The word froze on his lips.

In the bright beam of the car's headlights, the silhouettes of two houses were as clear and sharp as a cardboard cut-out. The Rigid-Smythe's house, No. 33, was exactly as they had left it. Neat and tidy. The problem was the house next door, the one Dudley was buying with his new partner Sid Bouncer. The one that was going to make them both millionaires after they turned it into flats.

This house now looked like a film-set for a second-rate horror movie.

A lopsided tower stuck out of a roof which was edged with battlements. Where the front lawn had once been there was a dark tangle of overgrown trees. You could just make out a tunnel cut through the hanging branches and lit with firebrands. Dudley's stomach filled with ice and then turned over slowly. Something had gone terribly wrong. Beside him, Pamela moaned gently, shook her head twice then didn't move again. It was as if she was stuck to the front seat.

A minute later Dudley got out and lifted his precious golf bag down from the roof rack. Now his game of golf with Sid Bouncer was more important than ever.

They had to come up with a plan fast.

Simon and Pearl jumped out of the car. They stood and looked up at the house next to theirs. Simon's mouth was the shape of a great big O. Ruby's mouth had turned into an enormous grin. Dudley leant his golf bag against the car and went round to the other side. Pamela had slumped to the floor.

****

Hidden behind the battlements of No. 34, Anaconda and Boris watched their new neighbours arrive. What sweet-looking children, thought Anaconda to herself. Then her eyes fastened on the golf bag Dudley had leaned against the car.

'Boris,' whispered Anaconda. 'Look at that fabulous snake carrier!'

In the dark night, Anaconda's eyes danced like purple flames.

'Everything is going to be perfect, Boris,' she cried happily. 'I just know it!'

Chapter Four

Pearl Wolfbane lay back in her princess's bed with its gauzy hangings. On the other side of the room an early morning sun shone through the pink and white striped curtains at her window.

Outside, the sweet notes of birdsong mixed with the deep croaks of bullfrogs. It was the most beautiful music Pearl thought she had ever heard.

Pearl heaved herself up on her pillows and let her eyes wander sleepily around her new bedroom. The walls were papered with a pattern of bows and seashells and edged with a border of deep, rosy pink. Under the window stood a dressing table with a skirt of shiny cotton printed with the same pattern as the wallpaper.

An oval mirror sat on top surrounded by sparkly hair bands and flower-shaped hair slides. In front of the dressing table was a stool covered in white velvet. It matched a delicate button-backed chair in the corner next to Pearl's collection of china mermaids.

Pearl swung out of bed and dug her toes into the thick creamy carpet that covered the floor. She pulled on her favourite silky dressing gown and crossed the room to open her curtains.

Pearl's room was at the front of the house. Ever since she had arrived at Primrose Drive, she had got up early in the morning, opened her window and leaned out over the sill to gaze down the road at the neat tidy gardens sparkling in the dawn dew.

Pearl sighed happily. Everything about her new house was perfect. She didn't even mind about the towers and battlements her mother and father had built because her parents had never seemed happier.

There was only one thing that Pearl missed in her new house and that was other children. There didn't seem to be any on Primrose Drive.

At that moment, Pearl turned to look at the house next door. She was expecting it to be shut-up and empty as usual.

It wasn't.

Pearl then found herself staring at a bicycle lying on its side in the road. It wasn't just any kind of bicycle. It was exactly the model Pearl had asked for at her last birthday. It had shiny silver handlebars with pale pink mudguards, a white leather seat and matching saddle-bags.

Pearl looked over the jungle of trees and bushes that Anaconda had planted at her own front gate. The bike she had actually been given was leaning against their white picket fence.

It was a black, rusty, three-wheeler that made a terrible creaking noise when you rode it.

Of course, Anaconda and Boris had been delighted with Pearl's present. They had searched every junk shop to find it. What's more, even though Boris had completely overhauled the bike, he had made sure the creaking noise stayed exactly the same.

Pearl turned and quickly pulled on a pair of candy striped trousers. The first thing she had to do was find out who was the owner of the shiny new bike.

At that moment she heard a particular CREAK! Only one thing made that noise! Her own rusty three-wheeler!

Pearl dragged a T-shirt over her head and ran back to the window. What she saw made her heart pound like a hammer.

A girl Pearl's age was standing beside her old bike. She had a heart-shaped face that was the colour of chalk and her thick, black hair was cut in a ragged fringe. It looked as if she closed her eyes and cut around her hair with pinking shears.

Which was exactly how Anaconda cut her own hair. Although sometimes she used garden shears if she felt like a change.

But the strangest thing of all was the way the girl was staring at Pearl's bike. She looked as if she wanted the rusty old bike more than anything else in the world.

Two minutes later, Pearl was standing in Clod's bedroom.

'Clod!' she shouted. 'Wake up!'

High above her in a camouflage-coloured hammock slung from the rafters, Clod Wolfbane grunted and stirred.

There was no printed wallpaper in Clod's room. There wasn't even any plasterboard on the walls. Clod had stripped everything down to the bare brick and floorboards. Then he had made shelves out of planks and concrete blocks all around the room. Then he had crammed every shelf with metal cages. Each cage contained a hairy spider, a shiny scorpion or a scuttling lizard.

Pearl pulled a face. She had never understood how Clod could hold huge spiders in his hands or let scorpions creep up his arms. But then Clod couldn't understand how she could collect china mermaids or like dressing-up.

Underneath Clod's hammock was a trampoline, which he used instead of a ladder to get up to bed. Pearl climbed onto it and began to bounce.

Four bounces later, she poked the lump in the hammock that was her brother.

'Clod! GET UP! We've got neighbours!'

Clod sat up with a jerk. 'Neighbours?' he shouted. 'Why didn't you say so?'

As Pearl somersaulted off the trampoline, Clod rolled out of his hammock. Then he bounced twice and landed on his feet in front of his sister.

Pearl grinned. It was no surprise to her that Clod slept in his clothes.

Ten minutes later, Clod and Pearl were climbing through the thick branches of an oak tree that separated the two gardens.

'Are you sure this is a good idea?' muttered Pearl. 'What happens if they see us spying on them? They might think we're weird.'

Somewhere hidden in the leaves, Clod chuckled. 'So what? It doesn't matter.'

But it did matter to Pearl.

She decided to have a quick peek then climb back down and go around and introduce herself like normal people do.

At that moment, Pearl pushed through a cluster of leaves and for the first time she saw the whole of their new neighbours' back garden.

Pearl couldn't believe her eyes! At the end of a beautifully mown lawn with flower-beds on either side was a sparkling blue swimming pool. There was even a little wooden pool hut that looked just like a doll's house! It was exactly like Felicity's surprise pool in *Felicity – A Happy Girl's Story*!

'Wow!' cried Pearl out loud. 'What a fantastic swimming pool!'

'If you like that sort of thing.'

Pearl froze. The voice was deep and scratchy. It didn't sound like Clod at all. Pearl felt every hair on the back of her neck stand up. She turned and found herself staring into the chalky face of the girl she had seen from her window.

'I like your water hole much better,' said the girl. Her coal-black eyes glittered and her face was almost angry. 'And I think your bike is brilliant.'

Pearl was so taken aback she said the first thing that came into her head.

'I wanted a bike like yours and I think your swimming pool is brilliant!'

For a moment neither girl spoke.

31

Then they both burst out laughing.

'My name's Ruby,' said the dark-haired girl. She didn't sound angry anymore. 'Ruby Rigid-Smythe.'

'Mine's Pearl,' said Pearl. 'Pearl Wolfbane.'

At that moment Clod's head dropped between them. He was hanging upside down from the branch above. 'Hi. I'm Clod, Pearl's brother.'

Ruby laughed. 'I've got a brother too,' she said. 'He's called Simon.'

'Far out!' cried Clod. He dropped on to the branch beside his sister.

'Where is he?'

Ruby shrugged. 'Asleep, I guess.'

Clod grinned. 'Why don't you wake him up and I'll cook toadburgers for breakfast?'

Pearl went bright red. 'Clod!' she cried. 'How can you talk about toadburgers? You'll make Ruby feel sick.'

'No, he won't,' said Ruby. 'I've heard of toadburgers. They're just like chicken but better!'

She laughed. 'And Simon will eat anything!'

'Okay,' said Pearl, seeing she was outnumbered. 'We'll have a breakfast picnic in our tree house!'

She shot a glance at Clod. 'Toadburgers are optional.'

'Anything you say,' said Clod. 'I'll go and put the kettle on.'

Then he climbed down through the branches and disappeared.

Pearl was expecting Ruby to go, too. But Ruby didn't move. Instead she sat and pulled apart a leaf in her hand. Suddenly Pearl's stomach was full of butterflies. Maybe she'd said something wrong. Maybe Ruby didn't want to have a picnic breakfast after all.

Pearl bit her lip. To her horror she felt her throat tightening and tears rising in her eyes. She was so looking forward to having friends next door. 'It doesn't matter if Simon doesn't like toadburgers,' said Pearl helplessly. She shrugged. 'I mean, I don't.'

Ruby dropped the leaf and looked into Pearl's clear blue eyes. 'I wasn't even thinking about toadburgers,' she said. 'I was thinking about your tree house. We've always wanted a tree house.'

To Pearl's amazement, she saw the glitter of tears in Ruby's eyes, too.

'But tree houses are easy to build,' cried Pearl. 'Just ask your dad to put up the frame.'

Ruby ripped up her leaf and watched it fall to the ground.

'We've asked our dad hundreds of times,' she muttered. 'He always says no.'

Because as far as Dudley was concerned, a tree house ruined a tidy garden. What's more it was too dangerous.

For some reason that Pearl didn't quite understand, she put out her hand and patted Ruby's arm.

'It doesn't matter if you don't have your own tree house,' she said gently. 'You and Simon can share ours.'

Chapter Five

Simon Rigid-Smythe watched the morning sun climb steadily into the sky. He looked at his watch. He reckoned he had another forty-five minutes before his mother knocked on his door, walked in without waiting for an answer and tried to take his temperature.

It was a no-win situation. If Simon let his mother take his temperature and it was normal (as it always was) then Pamela would convince herself the thermometer was broken and get another one. (Her bedside drawer was full of them.) If Simon refused, Pamela would convince herself he was ill and trying to hide it from her.

Slowly, without making any noise, Simon opened his cupboard and dragged a trunk into the middle of the room. He took a key from around his neck and opened the lid.

There were two sections in the trunk. One was jam-packed with screwdrivers, pliers, hammers, wires, batteries and all kinds of motor parts. The other side was stacked with tiny working robots, programmed to do anything Simon wanted them to do. Some picked up bits of paper and fluff from under his bed. Others sharpened his pencils. One even polished his shoes. And one – Simon was particularly proud of this one – was programmed to find missing socks.

Simon grinned to himself and picked up the robot he was working on. No one knew what was inside this trunk except for Ruby. His parents thought it was full of bits and pieces for the model train set that Dudley had put up in the attic. And perhaps there were a few rails or half a dozen iron wheels that might fit the trains. Simon didn't know or care because Dudley wouldn't let anyone else play with the set except himself. Besides, what Simon liked best of all was building things from scratch. So he wasn't really interested in his father's fancy toy engines.

The truth was that Simon Rigid-Smythe was a mechanical genius. And the only one who knew it was Ruby.

At that moment there were two sharp taps on the door. It was Ruby's signal. Simon replied with a low whistle and Ruby came into the room. Her face was flushed and excited.

'Hurry!' she whispered. 'We've been invited to a breakfast picnic in a tree house!'

Simon opened his mouth to speak but Ruby pointed towards their parents' bedroom and drew a finger across her neck. Simon nodded. She didn't have to explain. It was important to get up and get out fast before their parents woke up and found an excuse to say no.

So while Simon packed up his trunk and pushed it back in the cupboard, Ruby rolled up a blanket and stuffed it into Simon's bed. Now if their mother poked her head around the door it would look as if Simon was still asleep.

****

'A picnic breakfast!' crowed Anaconda again and again. 'What a wonderful idea!'

In front of her a large, wicker basket was packed to the brim with toadburgers, mangoes, crunchy chocolate beetles, sweet toffee snakes and a huge stripy watermelon.

'Ruby's gone to fetch Simon,' cried Pearl in a high, excited voice. She danced from foot to foot as she stuffed in a bottle of fresh orange juice, half a dozen buns and a jar of raspberry jam. 'She's really nice, Mum. I'm so glad they live next door.'

Boris looked up from the newspaper he was reading as he hung upside down from the ceiling.

'I knew you'd make friends,' he said wisely.

Boris believed that the longer you hung upside down, the cleverer you became. Something to do with your face getting redder and redder. This also meant that it was his habit to do the crossword only after he had read the paper from cover to cover and his face was purple.

'Everything's ready!'

Clod's face appeared at the door. He looked flushed and happy. 'I'll be at the tree house!'

Pearl picked up the wicker basket and ran up the stone stairs into the sunlight.

'Oh, Boris,' cried Anaconda. 'I'm so excited! Our first new neighbours!'

Boris's face was now almost black.

'Anaconda!' he cried. 'I've just had the most brilliant idea.'

Boris flipped backwards and landed lightly on the stone floor.

'Let's invite our new neighbours to a flesh roast by the mud hole!'

Boris grinned and took his wife in his arms. 'Isn't that what other people do?'

'Oh, Boris!' cried Anaconda as they danced and spun like tops around the room. 'I do believe it is!'

****

Five minutes later Simon Rigid-Smythe stood on his own at the bottom of the tree house. Ruby had shot up the rope ladder as soon as they had arrived. But it was as if Simon was frozen to the spot. Because Simon wasn't the only one who collected broken bits and pieces. Clod collected things, too. And kept them in a pile underneath the tree house.

So far Clod had found three rusty lawn mowers, a couple of broken-up cars, a set of racing car wheels, an old motorboat engine and various lengths of steel rails and iron bars.

'Wow!' Simon kept muttering to himself as he saw yet another piece of scrap glittering in the long grass. 'Wow. Oh, wow!'

And all the while Clod was hiding in the leaves watching him. It wasn't that Clod was spying, he was hiding because even though he looked and acted tough, the truth was that Clod was really very shy. And now that Ruby and Pearl were such good friends, Clod was hoping with all his might that he and Simon would be good friends, too.

But when he had seen Simon creeping through the long grass, he had been worried. Simon looked so pale and thin and he moved almost as slowly as a stick insect. Clod spent most of his time crashing about like a pinball in an arcade machine.

How could they possibly have anything at all in common?

As Clod watched Simon's face he suddenly knew he had nothing to worry about. It wasn't that Simon moved slowly. It was more that he moved carefully. As Clod watched Simon staring at the junk on the ground, he suddenly realized that Simon noticed everything.

Clod grabbed hold of a vine and swung down to the grass.

'I'm Clod,' he said, holding out his hand.

'I'm Simon,' said Simon. He shook Clod's hand. Then he rubbed his eyes as if he had just woken up from a dream. 'Is this your junk?'

'Yup,' said Clod, proudly.

A big smile spread across Simon's face.

'Ever thought of building an aeroplane?'

Chapter Six

Pamela Rigid-Smythe groaned from under her eye mask and rearranged the custom-made ice pack over her forehead. She had never known such awful nightmares. All night she had tossed and turned. And it was always the same terrible dream.

They had come back from their holiday to find the next door house had been turned into something that looked like a stage-set on a horror movie. Even worse, she dreamed she had sleepwalked over to the next door garden. In the cold light of dawn, where once there had been a neat lawn with tidy flowerbeds, she had seen a huge mud hole, filled with scummy, brown water and wriggling with snakes.

'Dudley,' she croaked. 'Headache. Weak tea. Headache. Weak tea.'

She reached out a pale arm to nudge her husband awake. Her hand flapped about on the other side of the bed. First it flapped around the pillow. Then it flapped up and down all over the duvet.

There was no one there! Pamela Rigid-Smythe sat up and ripped the mask from her eyes.

'Dudley!' she shrieked. 'Where are you?'

Dudley appeared from inside their His 'n' Hers walk-in wardrobe. He was dressed in red and green chequered plus fours, long yellow socks, a white polo shirt and a pale yellow v-necked sweater. In his right hand, he held his brand-new golfing gloves.

'Dudley!' shrieked Pamela. 'You can't leave me!'

She buried her head in her hands. 'I'm very delicate this morning.'

Dudley's hand shook as he poured out two cups of weak tea from the tea-making machine on the bedside table. Dudley was feeling more than somewhat delicate himself. That morning, he had woken earlier than his wife and had decided to have a proper look next door. After all it was possible that after such a long journey, maybe they had just been seeing things, like travellers see lakes in deserts. But lakes are just what are needed in deserts. And travellers always want to see them.

The house Dudley looked at was straight out of a Dracula movie. It made him feel sick to look at it. And the more Dudley looked at it, the sicker he felt. Because in Dudley's mind, he and Sid already owned No. 34. In fact they had already turned it into lots of flats and he was already a millionaire. Now everything was ruined because of some B-movie-crazed lunatic!

Dudley felt his hands clench into fists. He wanted to punch something. He wanted to lie down on the floor and kick. Quite apart from the house, all the plans he had so carefully worked out for that morning were wrecked as well. Because Dudley had worked out a subtle strategy. After he had beaten Sid at golf, he would soften the defeat by telling Sid that he was ready to go forward with the plan.

Since Dudley knew Sid wanted to get things going as soon as possible, he had emptied his savings account and put the money in a safe in the sitting room downstairs. It was the sort of thing powerful, clever businessmen did all the time, Dudley told himself smugly. Then he groaned out loud. What was the point in even bothering to think like this? He must be mad. All his plans were useless now.

Beside him, Pamela gulped her tea like a rabbit sucking from a water tube.

'I had horrible dreams about the house next door,' she whispered. 'I dreamt—'

Dudley Rigid-Smythe touched his wife's arm. 'They weren't dreams, dearest,' he whispered in a squeaking, shaking voice. 'That's why I have to keep my golf appointment with Sid Bouncer.'

Pamela looked at her husband's pink, staring eyes. He sounded like a madman. His hands were clenched into fists. He kept running his tongue round and round his lips. Even though she was unwell herself, Pamela made a huge effort and sat up. She grabbed a temperature strip from her bedside drawer.

'No, no,' cried Dudley. He pushed away the slimy, little strip his wife was waving at him. 'I don't have a temperature!' he almost screamed.

Dudley Rigid-Smythe tipped the contents of the sugar bowl into his tea and tried to lift the cup to his mouth.

It was no good. His hand was shaking too much. He put the cup back on the table and took a deep breath.

'The reason I have to meet Sid Bouncer,' said Dudley as if he was trying not to scream, 'is because Sid Bouncer knows everyone. He is a powerful man.'

Pamela Rigid-Smythe groaned. She could feel a dull throb return to her temples.

'Sid Bouncer will know what to do about the people who have moved in next door,' said Dudley as if he was reciting something by heart. 'He'll know the right man in the Mayor's office. That man will convince these people to leave.'

This time Dudley picked his cup up using both hands and managed to raise it right up to his mouth. He had finally reached the part that made him feel better. 'Then everything will go ahead, just as I'd planned.'

Images from her dream flashed through Pamela's mind. A lopsided tower, crumbling battlements, a tangled jungle, an enormous mud hole. A terrible realization washed over her.

'So it's all true?' she croaked.

Without another word, Pamela Rigid-Smythe sank back against her pillows and pulled the sheet over her head.

****

On the other side of town in a caravan next to a used-car garage, Sid Bouncer was also getting ready for his game of golf. Sid had things on his mind, too. But they were very different from

Dudley's. Sid twisted a cravat neatly around his neck and fixed it in place with a diamond tie-pin. Then he pulled on a daffodil-yellow cashmere sweater and straightened it over his perfectly pressed golfing trousers.

Of the many things Sid knew, one of the most important was to look the part. And today Sid had to look exactly right because he was playing a very important part.

Next to him a woman in a gold dressing-gown stretched out her long legs (even though there wasn't a lot of room in the caravan) and then began to paint her toenails scarlet.

'Do you think he'll go for it, Sid?' murmured Goldie Bouncer as she moved smoothly from one toe to the next. 'Dudley might not be as stupid as he looks.'

Sid Bouncer pulled up a picture in his mind of Dudley Rigid-Smythe's smug smile and shiny, brown eyes.

'Of course he'll go for it,' said Sid. 'He thinks he's a clever businessman.'

Sid slipped into a pair of expensive golfing shoes he had stolen from someone else's locker at the Club the week before. Then he straightened his sweater for the last time and examined his reflection in the mirror. He looked like a smooth-shaven warthog with slicked-back, black hair.

'And if we're really lucky,' Sid continued, 'he'll be stupid enough to have the money in a safe in his house.'

Goldie Bouncer stood up and flicked an imaginary hair off Sid's shoulder. 'I'm good at finding safes,' she said. A wolfish grin spread across her face. 'Why don't we all meet up for a friendly little drink quite soon.'

Sid smiled and kissed his wife on her forehead. 'Anything you say, sweetest.'

Sid and Goldie Bouncer were a team. And they always worked in the same way. First Sid would join a golf club in a new area and look out for a sucker with a high opinion of himself. Then Goldie would appear and chat up the wife. Soon the two couples would be the best of friends. And that was the moment that Sid would come up with a business deal that would make them both millionaires. It was always the same sort of scam. Buying a house and converting it into flats. But this time, it couldn't have been easier because the house Sid had suggested was the house next door to Dudley.

Goldie handed Sid the pair of brand-new, golfing gloves she had stolen last week.

'Make sure you let him win,' she said. 'It'll make him think he's smarter than you.'

Chapter Seven

Three hours later, Sid swirled the ice cubes in his long glass and leaned back on a padded deck chair in the Rigid-Smythe's garden.

'You worry too much, Dudley,' said Sid smoothly. 'Your neighbours are doing us a favour. The place will be even cheaper once they go.'

'But how do you know they'll go?' asked Pamela in a choked voice.

Goldie smiled and patted Pamela's hand. 'Don't you worry, dear,' she murmured. 'Sid looks after these things.'

'I certainly do,' agreed Sid, holding out his glass for a refill. 'Leave it to me.' He grinned roguishly.

For the first time since they had come back from holiday, Dudley Rigid-Smythe was beginning to feel better. Not only had he easily beaten Sid at golf, it also seemed that his plans weren't ruined, after all. At any rate, Dudley knew his part of the deal was ready and packed in a briefcase in the safe inside. And Sid was right. It was his job to find a way of encouraging the new neighbours to leave. Dudley thought about what Sid had said on the golf course.

'Forewarned is forearmed, old man. Know your enemy. It's half the battle.'

'Mum. Dad. This is Pearl. She's our new next-door neighbour.'

All four adults froze. Pamela Rigid-Smythe almost dropped the drink she was holding.

Ruby was standing next to a little girl who couldn't have looked more different from her. She had blonde hair and clear blue eyes and her clothes were neat and tidy. She didn't look at all like the kind of girl who would live in a crumbling castle and swim in a mud hole. But it wasn't the difference between the two girls that startled Pamela. It was the look on Ruby's face. For the first time, Ruby looked completely happy.

'How lovely to meet you, Pearl,' said Pamela quickly trying to recover herself.

'This is, uh, Dudley, Ruby's father, and, uh, Sid and Goldie Bouncer.'

'Hello.'

Pearl smiled her lovely smile and her clear blue eyes sparkled. 'We've been hoping we'd have neighbours ever since we arrived.'

'And, uh, what have you two been up to all day?' asked Pamela, who had just realized she hadn't seen her daughter for most of the day.

'We've had a brilliant time, Mum,' cried Ruby. 'First we had breakfast in Clod and Pearl's tree house, then we went out on our bikes.'

Ruby laughed out loud. 'And we swapped because I like Pearl's bike better than mine!'

Dudley smiled and ruffled his daughter's ragged black hair. 'I suppose it's this year's model.'

'Oh, no!' Ruby shook her head. 'It's an old black three-wheeler with an amazing creak.'

Pearl saw a peculiar look pass between the Bouncers and the Rigid-Smythes. She blushed and looked at her feet because she knew immediately that the grown-ups been talking about her family a moment before.

'Pearl's parents searched endless junk shops for it,' continued Ruby proudly. 'And Anaconda—'

Pamela Rigid-Smythe's hand flew to her mouth. 'Have they got snakes?'

Pearl felt her stomach turn over. It was the way Ruby's mother said 'they'.

'Anaconda is my mother's name,' murmured Pearl.

'Pearl's mum wears these fantastic swirly black dresses,' cried Ruby. 'And her dad hangs upside down in the kitchen like a bat!'

Pearl's blush went from pink to red.

'And Simon and Clod are making something top secret!'

'Simon?' squawked Pamela Rigid-Smythe. 'I thought he was still asleep.'

'Who's Clod?' asked Dudley nervously.

'Sounds like a lump of earth to me,' squawked Goldie Bouncer.

'Clod is Pearl's brother,' replied Ruby, coldly. She didn't like Goldie Bouncer one little bit. 'He's got an amazing junk collection.'

She paused and looked at her mother. 'And Simon really likes him.'

Poor Pearl. She wished the ground would open and swallow her up.

'I'd better go home now,' she whispered to Ruby.

'What?' Ruby almost shouted. 'But Pearl, I was going to show you my room.'

Forewarned is forearmed. Dudley forced a smile onto his face. Almost imperceptibly, Sid Bouncer winked at him.

'Of course you must see Ruby's room, Pearl,' said Dudley smoothly. 'She's very proud of it.'

Pamela Rigid-Smythe took her cue from her husband. She turned to Pearl with a sugary-sweet smile.

'And if Clod would like to come over with Simon—'

'Simon likes it at Clod's house, Mum,' said Ruby simply.

And before Pamela could reply, she took Pearl by the arm and led her into the kitchen. At first Pearl couldn't believe what she was looking at. She had seen all kinds of kitchens but never one like this. The walls were panelled and were painted pale green. All the cupboards and drawers were hidden. There were no cups or plates or knives and forks to be seen anywhere. Even the sink was hidden under a sliding counter. Even stranger, there was no sign of food. A round table stood in the middle of the room but it was completely empty except for two green salt and pepper pigs which were some of the ugliest things Pearl had even seen in her life.

Ruby yanked open a green panel by the door. It turned into a fridge. She reached behind stacks of different-sized food containers and eased out two cans of orangeade. Then she slammed the door shut and Pearl followed her into the hall. Through the open doors, Pearl could see every room had the same sort of feel as the kitchen.

Suddenly she realized that all the things she took for granted were missing. There were no paintings or books. There were no hangings or bunches of flowers. In fact there was no clutter at all. The whole house had the feel of a show home. It was furnished, carpeted and curtained but it was as if no one lived there.

Then Pearl saw something that looked like a large, gold grate except it had carved sides and was fixed halfway up the wall. It was completely different from everything else and the only thing that looked as if the Rigid-Smythes had chosen it themselves. Pearl stopped.

'What's that?'

Ruby pulled a face. 'It's a safe.' She walked over to the wall, pushed what looked like an ordinary light switch and the gold grate swung open.

Pearl stared at the iron box that was fitted into the wall. It had a round combination lock surrounded by numbers. She'd read about these locks hundreds of times but she'd never seen one.

'Does it click when you turn it round?'

A mischievous smile played on Ruby's face. She went over to the safe and turned the knob backwards and forwards. Five turns later, there was a loud CLICK and the safe door opened.

'Ruby!' gasped Pearl. 'You shouldn't!'

Ruby peered inside. 'Nothing there but a boring old briefcase,' she muttered. Then she shut the safe door and pushed the gold grate back against the wall. At the window, a curtain fluttered in the breeze. Except there was no wind that day.

It was Goldie Bouncer's hand trembling with excitement.

A minute later, Pearl stood in the middle of Ruby's room trying to think of something to say. The walls and the ceilings were painted pitch black and covered in crazy-looking fish. Some floated in midair, attached to see-through string from the ceiling. It was as if they were a thousand feet beneath the surface of the ocean. Suddenly Pearl realized that her room must have seemed as weird to Ruby as Ruby's room now seemed to her.

Pearl thought of something her father had said one day after he had been hanging upside down for a long time. 'If it makes you happy, dear, who cares?'

'So,' demanded Ruby almost fiercely. 'What do you think?'

Pearl turned to Ruby. 'Amazing,' she said, 'but—'

'But what?'

Pearl laughed uneasily. Suddenly she felt confused. 'It's so different from everything I've seen in your house.'

'That's because my parents are weird.'

'What!' Pearl couldn't believe her ears. 'It's my parents that are weird, not yours.'

Ruby threw herself down on a beanbag. 'Your parents are weird, too, but they're weird in a good way.'

Ruby bit her lip. 'At least they don't mind if people are different from them.'

Ruby's eyes went hot and dark. 'All my parents care about is being the same or even better than everyone else,' she muttered. 'They hate anyone who's different from them.'

Pearl sighed. She thought of Boris and Anaconda – they were so desperate to get to know people. They didn't care if people did things in different ways. All they wanted was for everyone to be happy. 'So your parents wouldn't like my parents.'

Ruby nodded miserably. 'The truth is they're probably frightened of your parents even though they haven't even met them.'

And before she could stop it, a big tear ran down her face. Pearl grabbed Ruby's hand. 'Don't cry,' she whispered. 'We'll make them be friends.'

Chapter Eight

'Crave!' muttered Anaconda. 'That's a good word.' She picked up a quill pen, and began writing her loopy, old-fashioned scrawl across another sheet of parchment.

'We crave your companionship for nibbles.' Anaconda looked up. 'What do you think, Boris?'

Boris swung back and forth humming gently to himself. 'No, dear,' he muttered. 'I don't think crave is right at all.'

'I give up!'

Anaconda scrunched up the paper into a ball and threw it on the floor. It was as if a storm of giant hailstones had blown in through the kitchen door. Everything was covered with crunchy paper balls.

'You do it!' cried Anaconda.

'Do what?' asked Clod.

Anaconda spun round. Boris flipped backwards and landed neatly on the floor. Clod was standing beside a pale, thin boy with a shock of red hair. At first Anaconda thought the boy must be ill, he was so pale. Then she noticed his eyes. They sparkled like emeralds. It was as if they were lit up by a light bulb inside his head.

'Mum, Dad. This is Simon,' said Clod. 'He lives next door.'

Simon smiled shyly. 'Hello.'

Anaconda bounded across the room with one swinging stride. 'Simon!' she cried. 'How wonderful that you are here in my kitchen just as I have made something truly delicious, which I think you will really like!'

'Good to see you, Simon,' said Boris. He took Simon's hand firmly in his. 'Please sit down and join us.'

Five minutes later Simon found himself munching lumps of delicious pink cake and sipping Boris's homemade chameleon cordial. He had never felt so happy in all his life.

'Of course, it's not made of real chameleons,' Boris was saying. 'I call it chameleon cordial because it changes colour when you think different thoughts.'

Boris laughed. 'Just one of my little experiments.'

Simon was amazed. He felt so at ease with Clod's parents that he began to tell them all about his robots.

'Simon's a genius,' said Clod through a mouthful of pink cake. He gulped at his cordial. It turned sky blue. 'We're building an – oops! I forgot – it's a secret.'

'Only until it's ready,' said Simon quickly. His cordial had turned silver, striped with red. 'Then everyone will know.'

'How exciting,' cried Anaconda. 'I love secrets!'

'Why?' asked Simon, helping himself to another piece of pink cake.

'Because secrets can turn into wonderful surprises!' crowed Anaconda happily – which is when she had a brainwave. 'Would your parents like to come to a surprise celebration?'

At the mention of his parents, Simon nearly choked on his cake. He suddenly remembered he hadn't seen them all day.

'I – uh.' Suddenly Simon didn't know what to say. It was as if the mention of his parents had broken a magical spell.

'That settles it,' cried Anaconda, mistaking his silence for shyness. 'I shall invite them!' She picked up a quill pen and began to scratch a note across a piece of parchment:

Come to a surprise supper,

your new neighbours Boris and Anaconda Wolfbane.

Anaconda waved her arms about. 'Would they prefer to eat inside in the subterranean dining area or outside by the roasted flesh charpit?'

At the mention of roasted flesh, Boris remembered what he'd read about getting to know people. 'Let's eat outside,' he cried. 'Then we can all have a dip in the mud hole!'

****

And that was how later that afternoon Pamela and Dudley Rigid-Smythe found themselves creeping through a leafy green tunnel up to the Wolfbanes' front door. Ruby and Simon had gone over earlier. To help get things ready, they said. But the truth was they both wanted to be with their new neighbours as much as possible.

As Pamela brushed a velvety leaf from her cheek, she couldn't help thinking about Simon when he had come home carrying the Wolfbanes' invitation. His face had looked shiny and pink, not dull and white. Somehow he even seemed to have grown and filled out. As for Ruby, Pamela was still stunned by the change in her daughter. She couldn't remember the last time Ruby had smiled, let alone laughed. Now there was a brightness and enthusiasm about her that Pamela realized she had never seen before.

For the first time, tiny doubts about their deal with Sid Bouncer began to prickle at the edges of Pamela's perfectly-formed brain. What right did she and Dudley have to interfere in the lives of a family whose tastes happened to be different from theirs? It wasn't as if they needed the money. Pamela forced herself to confront the truth. It was greed and fear that was behind their arrangement with Sid Bouncer. Suddenly Pamela's doubts turned into a cold, sick feeling in her stomach. What if Ruby and Simon ever found out that it was their own parents who had forced their new friends and neighbours out? Pamela groaned.

'They would never forgive us!' she muttered out loud.

Dudley turned sharply towards her. 'What?'

He had been lost in his own thoughts, thinking the same thing over and over again. Forewarned is forearmed. Forewarned is forearmed.

'What did you say?'

'Nothing,' murmured Pamela miserably.

'Greetings, neighbours!' cried Boris.

Pamela and Dudley found themselves looking into a long, smiling face with a hooked nose and eyes that glowed like coals.

'Boris Wolfbane! At your service!'

He grasped Dudley's hand. It felt about as firm as a wet fish.

'Please call me Boris! My friends call me nothing else!'

'Dudley Rigid-Smythe,' muttered Dudley stiffly. 'Pamela, my wife.'

Boris took Pamela's cool skinny hand in his.

'Delighted,' crowed Boris. His eyes glittered. 'Follow me! Anaconda awaits us!'

As Pamela and Dudley followed Boris down the corridor, they both had the oddest sensation. Even though No. 34 Primrose Drive was roughly the same size as No. 33, the corridor was more like a castle hallway. Through open doors, they could see huge rooms hung with portraits and glittering with glass and dark polished furniture. Boris smiled a Cheshire cat's smile.

'We made a few little changes when we arrived,' he murmured. 'Makes it seem more homely, don't you think?'

'Y-y-yes,' stammered Dudley as he passed a trampoline standing beside an enormous suit of armour. He looked up and saw that many of the floorboards had been taken away, leaving rafters that criss-crossed the house like ribs.

'So much faster than using the stairs,' explained Boris.

Butterflies fluttered through Dudley's stomach. It was almost as if this man could read his thoughts. Dudley was all the more determined to be on his guard.

At that moment Anaconda swept up from what appeared to be a cave in the ground. She was holding a silver tray with four tall, delicately-carved glasses. Behind her Pearl and Ruby were giggling and chatting as they carried up plates of tiny black and red tarts. And Simon and Clod joked and laughed as they manhandled a huge crystal bowl filled with a shimmering rainbow punch up the stairs.

Again Pamela was struck by the change in her children. She tried to catch Dudley's eye to see if he had noticed it, too. But Dudley was staring fixedly at a large, yellow frog swimming slowly across the green, scummy water in the mud hole in front of them.

Anaconda put down her tray and shook Pamela's hand. 'We're so pleased to meet you at last,' she cried. 'Ruby and Simon have told us so much about you!'

She smiled a sparkling smile at Dudley. 'I knew from the moment I saw your clever snake carrier that we would get on!'

'I beg your pardon?' muttered Dudley. Ruby threw back her head and laughed. 'Mrs Wolfbane means your golf club bag, Dad,' she explained.

'Of course I do!' Anaconda beamed as she poured out the shimmering liquid into four glasses. 'It's a family recipe,' she explained as Dudley and Pamela peered suspiciously at the glasses in their hands. 'It's for celebrations and special occasions.'

Anaconda flashed her sparkling smile and raised her glass. 'To wonderful things happening!'

'Truly wonderful things,' added Boris.

'Uh, yes,' said Dudley in a strangled voice and drained his glass to hide his embarrassment.

Anaconda immediately refilled it.

'Now, tell me about this golf,' she asked sweetly. 'Do you play it with hard snakes?'

Pamela Rigid-Smythe made a sound like a camel choking and gulped her own glass in one.

Boris smiled and refilled it.

Anaconda thought hard. What sort of thing would fit into a snake-shaped bag? Of course!

'Or do you use bones?'

Neither Pamela nor Dudley could speak. Ruby and Simon exchanged worried looks with Pearl and Clod. They were so desperate for their parents to get on that Clod had secretly raided Boris's experimental booze cupboard and poured half a bottle of GET ON GUMPTION that he'd found at the back into the punch. But things weren't going well at all. Clod pulled a face. Maybe the GET ON GUMPTION had gone stale.

'What are we going to do?' muttered Ruby helplessly.

Then Simon had a brainwave. If there was one thing his father couldn't resist, it was showing off his golf swing.

'I'll set up the practice net and bring over the clubs,' he shouted, a little too loudly. 'Dad can show Mrs Wolfbane how to swing.'

Anaconda clapped her hands. Everything seemed to be going so smoothly. It was lovely having neighbours.

'What a clever idea, Simon!' she cried. 'I adore swinging.'

At that moment, something extraordinary happened. It was so extraordinary that Ruby and Simon nearly fainted. Dudley burst out laughing.

'I'd be delighted to show you my swing.'

Boris topped up Pamela's half-empty glass.

'Do you like golf, Pamela?' he asked.

Pamela felt an odd sensation play around her

lips. It was something she hadn't felt for a very long time. Then she started laughing, too.

'I hate golf,' she chortled. 'It's really, really boring.'

'Pamela!' gasped Dudley. 'You never told me that!'

Sobs of laughter shook Pamela's body. 'You never asked.'

While Simon fetched the clubs, Clod filled up the crystal bowl with more rainbow punch. Just for luck he tipped in the last of the GET ON GUMPTION. It did seem to be working, after all!

Half an hour later, Dudley was asking Anaconda's advice on his golf swing because it turned out that Anaconda was a complete natural and could hit a ball perfectly every time.

'You must join the Golf Club,' muttered Dudley again and again.

You MUST join the Golf Club!

Meanwhile Boris and Pamela were discussing garden design. Gardening was a great hobby of Boris's but the idea of putting flowers into beds had never occurred to him. Equally Pamela had never understood the gloriousness of jungles. Now she was strangely taken by Boris's techniques. Of course Ruby, Pearl, Clod and Simon had run off as soon as their parents had tucked into the second lot of rainbow punch.

Everything was going along beautifully.

Everything, that is, until there there was a huge SMASH of breaking glass.

****

Anaconda and Boris stood beside Pamela and Dudley and stared down at the floor in the sitting room at the front of the house. A large rock wrapped in heavy, brown paper lay in a pile of broken glass at their feet. Nobody spoke as Boris bent down and smoothed out the paper.

Words were scrawled across the paper in black, ugly letters:

GET OUT OR YOUR HOUSE BURNS DOWN. YOU HAVE BEEN WARNED.

All the worries in Pamela's mind that she had pushed away while she had been laughing and enjoying herself for the first time in a long time, suddenly rushed back. She turned to Dudley and opened her mouth as if she was trying to speak. Instead she let out a howl of despair and collapsed, sobbing, onto the floor.

Chapter Nine

'Almost finished,' muttered Simon from underneath the most extraordinary-looking aeroplane.

The body was made out of car panels, painted silver with a red stripe along its side. The wings were two thin lengths of wood covered in stretched canvas. The engine, which came out of an old sports car, was fixed to the front and attached to a rod that turned the propeller. Clod thought it was the most beautiful thing he had ever seen.

'One more turn.'

Simon picked up a large socket wrench and yanked it hard. Then he stood up and grinned all over his oily, black face.

'Let's give it a go!'

Clod could hardly breathe, he was so excited. 'Wait till they see us! Wait till they see us!' He had even brought a special camera so he could take a picture of everyone's amazed upturned faces. Clod let out a huge whoop of delight. 'They'll NEVER believe it!'

The two boys pushed the plane to the end of garden where there was a wide break in the hedge. On the other side of the hedge was a long field where the grass was smooth enough for the plane to take off.

'Ready?' Simon climbed into the pilot's seat, strapped up his seat-belt and put on a pair of old-fashioned goggles.

'Ready.'

Clod jumped in beside him and pulled on a pair of ski goggles. They both wore woolly hats, ski mitts, anoraks and long scarves wrapped around their necks. Simon crossed his fingers then turned the key of the old sports car engine. It started first go! In front of them the blades of the plane's propeller slowly started to turn.

'It works! It works!' shouted Simon.

'Yee-haw!' yelled Clod, punching his fist into the air.

The blades whirled round and round. When they were just a blur, Simon moved the joystick forward. There was a bump and lurch and the plane began to move. A moment later they were racing across the grass. Faster and faster and faster! Suddenly the plane shuddered and the ground beneath them disappeared! They were flying!

Clod felt the wind roar past his face as they climbed high over the treetops. The noise of the wind and the engine was so loud it was impossible to speak. Clod pulled out a tiny blackboard and scrawled a message with a piece of chalk:

FAR OUT!

Simon grinned and nodded. They flew above Primrose Drive, and turned to swoop over their parents' party. In the setting sun, the grey turrets of No. 34 Primrose Drive glittered gold and red. It looked like a castle surrounded by a thick, green, tangled jungle.

Suddenly something else glittered gold! Clod and Simon looked across to No. 33. It was Goldie Bouncer's yellow hair! Both boys watched as she climbed out of the sitting room window and ran after a man clutching a briefcase. The man was Sid Bouncer. In front of him, a red car with its front doors open was waiting in the road. Simon thought hc was going to be sick. He remembered what Ruby told him she'd seen in the safe. 'Nothing but a boring old briefcase,' she'd said.

But Simon knew it wasn't just a briefcase. It was the briefcase Dudley had taken with him when he had gone to the bank. In that split second Simon knew without a shadow of a doubt that Sid was stealing his father's money!

Even though Clod didn't know about the money in the briefcase, he could see that someone was stealing something from Simon's parents. As fast as he could, he pulled out his camera and took a picture. Then he scrawled three words on the tiny blackboard:

Follow the car.

Simon turned a wide circle as fast as he could at a safe distance, so that Sid and Goldie wouldn't suspect anything, then the little plane followed the red car as it wound through the streets and headed out of town. They flew over the golf course and the big houses that sat in the middle of large, leafy gardens where Sid had pretended to live. At last the red car stopped in front of a tiny caravan standing on its own beside a used-car garage.

Clod scribbled another note:
Home. FAST!

****

From the moment Pamela saw the smashed window and the message tied around the rock, she knew she and Dudley had made a terrible mistake.

Now she sat on the floor with her head in her hands. 'I'm so sorry,' she sobbed. 'I never ever thought Sid Bouncer would do something so horrible!'

A huge sigh passed through Pamela's body. 'Oh, Dudley. We've been so idiotic and unkind.'

She turned to Anaconda who had sat down beside her. 'Will you ever forgive us? Ruby and Simon would be so desperately unhappy if they knew how stupid we have been.'

'It's our fault, too,' Anaconda whispered. 'We didn't think our changes would upset you and that made things worse.'

She tried a small smile. 'But it's so wonderful that our children get on so well. Pearl and Clod have never had proper friends before.'

Pamela looked up through teary eyes. 'Nor have Ruby and Simon.'

'That settles it then,' said Anaconda firmly as she helped Pamela to her feet. 'The children must not be upset on any account.'

As Pamela had blurted out the whole sorry story, Dudley had stood silently. Just like his wife, Dudley had been absolutely appalled when he saw the message. Never in a million years would he have believed Sid could do something like that. For the first time in his life, Dudley felt so ashamed he wanted to do anything to put things right. So when Pamela finished speaking, Dudley told Boris everything from the moment Sid had first spoken to him at the golf course to the conversation they had had earlier that day.

Dudley shook his head miserably. 'The truth is I'm greedy and pig-headed and Sid Bouncer must have seen me coming.'

Boris took a match out of his pocket, picked up the bit of paper and set fire to it. Everyone watched as the flames curled around the ugly letters and destroyed them. Boris stamped out the burnt black pieces that fluttered to the floor. 'Let's just forget all about it,' he said kindly. 'It's all over now.'

'I hope so,' replied Dudley in a choked voice.

At that moment, Pearl, Ruby, Clod and Simon rushed into the room. Their faces were white and frightened.

'Something terrible's happened!' cried Simon. He looked at his sister as if he couldn't bear to say what it was.

'Sid Bouncer has stolen the briefcase from your safe!' cried Ruby.

Dudley rubbed his hands over his face. He felt as if he was sliding down a precipice.

'Are you sure about this?' asked Boris, turning to Clod.

Clod nodded.

'I even took a picture of them from the aeroplane we built.' He looked at his mother. 'That was the top-secret surprise we were making.'

Pamela Rigid-Smythe turned to Simon as if she was in a dream. Her eyes were round and staring.

'You were flying an aeroplane,' she whispered.

For the second time that day, Pamela sank to the floor.

Chapter Ten

'All my life's savings,' cried Dudley as he stared at the safe. 'He's stolen all my life's savings.'

Dudley slumped down on a chair. On the other side of the room, the gold grate was open and the safe was empty.

'Don't worry, Dudley dear,' said Anaconda brightly. 'We'll steal them back and everything will be normal again.'

'Normal!' cried Pamela. 'It was that stupid idea that got us into all this mess in the first place.'

Ruby was so surprised her eyes nearly popped out on stalks.

'But you want everyone to be normal,' she almost shouted.

Pamela looked at her daughter unhappily. 'Everyone makes mistakes,' she muttered.

Ruby couldn't believe what she was hearing. 'So you won't try to make me wear pretty-pink clothes anymore?'

'No more pretty-pink clothes,' replied her mother in a hollow voice.

Ruby narrowed her eyes. 'So I can give them to Pearl?'

'Ruby!' cried Pearl. 'I could never—'

'Oh, yes you could,' cried Ruby. 'I'll swap them for the ones you don't like that your mother keeps giving you!'

Now it was Anaconda's turn to be surprised. She looked at Pearl.

'You mean the old, black, velvet ones? I thought you liked the old, black, velvet ones.'

Pearl rolled her eyes. 'Mum,' she said in a patient voice. 'You think I like the specially-torn grey ones and designer-ripped purple ones.'

'Wow!' cried Ruby. 'I never thought I'd get excited about clothes!'

Everyone began to laugh.

'Excuse me, ladies,' said Boris firmly. 'Perhaps you can talk about clothes another time? We have more serious things to think about now.'

He turned to Dudley. 'Where does this Sid Bouncer live?'

'One of those big houses by the golf course,' replied Dudley miserably.

'No, he doesn't,' said Simon. 'He lives in a caravan next to a used-car garage.'

'We followed him in the aeroplane!' cried Clod.

Anaconda's eyes lit up. A plan was taking shape in her head.

'Why don't Clod and Simon keep watch from their aeroplane while the rest of us set off by road?' she said.

'But what if the Bouncers escape?' asked Pearl. 'How will we know?'

'My walkie-talkies!' shouted Clod suddenly. 'We'll have one and you'll have the other.'

'Brilliant idea, Clod,' cried Simon as Clod rushed out the door.

The tiniest spark of hope flickered in Dudley's eyes. 'We could all fit into my car,' he whispered.

Simon shook his head. 'I forgot to tell you. The tyres have all been let down.'

'Then we'll go in our carriage,' cried Boris. 'The horses could do with a gallop!'

Ten minutes later, Dudley found himself sitting beside Boris and clattering down Primrose Drive on top of the strangest carriage he had ever seen. It was black with spidery wheels encrusted in green scum. Inside, Pearl, Ruby, Anaconda and Pamela hadn't stopped talking from the moment they sat back on the buttoned velvet seats.

Dudley was amazed. Even though everything seemed to be going wrong, he was almost enjoying himself.

As the carriage turned out of Primrose Drive, there was a low roar overhead. A peculiar-looking aeroplane shot across the the sky in front of them. Simon and Clod waved furiously. Then the plane banked sharply and headed across the town.

'Your boy's a genius,' shouted Boris above the noise of the galloping hooves. 'You must be very proud of him.'

Dudley was desperately proud of Simon even though he had never been able to show it, let alone say it. Now he looked Boris in the face.

'I am proud of him,' shouted Dudley. 'And he makes a great team with Clod!'

'Excellent!' shouted Boris in reply. He shook the reins and the horses shot forward onto the main road.

It was odd, thought Dudley later. As they thundered across the town towards the golf course, he was barely aware of any other cars or indeed any other people on the road. For Dudley, it was the sort of journey where you start off as one person and end up another.

As trees and houses flashed past, Dudley thought about what had happened and couldn't believe he had been so awful. It was because he had been frightened. Frightened to appear different. Frightened not to fit in. Frightened to be left behind. And that had made him into someone who was mean, grasping and pretentious.

Dudley turned to Boris. He knew that he would understand without any explanation.

'You've given me a second chance! Thank you!'

Boris grinned. 'You've given it to yourself,' he shouted back.

'Silver Bird to Stagecoach! Silver Bird to Stagecoach!'

The walkie-talkie in Dudley's hand crackled into life. Dudley was so surprised he nearly fell off the seat. 'Come in, Silver Bird!'

'They've gone!' Clod's voice squawked. 'We've looked for them everywhere! What shall we do?'

Boris held out his hand for the walkie-talkie.

'Land and wait for us,' he shouted. 'We're almost there.'

Then to Dudley's amazement, a great grin spread across Boris's face.

'Don't give up,' he cried. 'Anaconda's got a nose like a bloodhound. They won't get far!'

Chapter Eleven

The tiny caravan looked like a hurricane had gone through it. There were bills, brochures and old clothes strewn about all over the place. While the children took turns flying about in the aeroplane, the adults crammed into the caravan and sat on the cramped seats. Anaconda examined everything she could see. Dudley watched as she picked up some expensive-looking golf shoes. She turned them over. They had obviously never been used. Dudley felt another wave of shame wash over him. It was obvious Sid had no idea how to play golf at all.

They watched Anaconda hold up some cheap jewellery that was stashed in a drawer as if she was trying to guess its weight. She was obviously looking for something or some things but she didn't yet know what they were. As she looked she put aside a tiny pile of objects. There was a letter from a travel agency and four leather address labels that had obviously come from four brand-new, matching suitcases.

Pamela stared as Anaconda began to sift through the hundreds of hotel brochures that were scattered on the floor. They came from all over the world. And they were all very, very fancy. Suddenly she pounced on one and jumped to her feet.

'Got 'em!' she cried, sounding very pleased with herself. 'They're flying to Spain tomorrow.'

Neither Dudley nor Pamela said anything. There was nothing to say. They were too late. Their life savings were gone. Sid and Goldie had pulled it off.

'But we're not too late!' crowed Anaconda triumphantly. 'There's a receipt here for a room at the Regency Ritz tonight! We'll dress up and trap 'em!'

****

Goldie Bouncer pulled on a brand-new gold-sequined evening dress she had bought especially for their last evening in England. She leaned forward and kissed her reflection in the long gilt-edged mirror on the wall of the penthouse suite at the Regency Ritz Hotel.

'Sid,' she murmured. 'I could get used to this.'

Sid Bouncer walked across the rich Persian carpet that covered the floor. He was dressed in a black evening suit with a rich purple cummerbund. His white shirt had ruffles edged with purple down the front.

He kissed his wife lightly on the cheek. 'You shall, my lovely,' he murmured. 'There are lots of fabulous hotels in Spain.'

Goldie fastened a thick gold chain, also brand-new, around her neck. 'Sid,' she whispered. 'Do you feel sorry for the... what were their names?'

'Rigid-Smythes,' replied Sid. 'And the answer is definitely no.'

'Fools and their money are soon parted,' giggled Goldie.

'Exactly.'

Sid clipped on a shiny purple bow tie. 'And a bigger fool than Dudley Rigid-Smythe, it hasn't been my privilege to meet.'

'Talking about money,' said Goldie. 'Where did you put the briefcase?'

'In the hotel safe,' replied Sid. 'It's the best place for it.'

****

Simon and Clod didn't care what clothes they wore to the Regency Ritz. And nobody else minded either as long as they wiped the grease off their faces. Simon put on a pair of clean overalls. Clod dug out some almost presentable jeans. It was a different story for Ruby and Pearl. It was Pearl's idea. 'We'll start as we mean to go on,' she whispered to Ruby as they rattled home in the carriage.

'What does that mean?' asked Ruby.

Pearl grinned. 'You choose from my clothes and I choose from yours!'

And so it happened that the Wolfbanes and the Rigid-Smythes almost jumped out of their skins when their daughters joined them as they were about to leave for the Regency Ritz.

Ruby looked sensational in Pearl's shredded black velvet skirt and designer-torn, gun-grey top. Pearl looked stunning in Ruby's lacy, silver party-dress with a matching bolero jacket and pale-blue, suede shoes.

Boris was delighted. 'You both look absolutely lovely,' he cried.

'Splendid,' said Dudley.

Anaconda wanted to pop open a bottle of champagne then and there.

But Boris said no. They were running out of time already and they still had to make two stops on the way to the Regency Ritz.

One at a camera film shop called 'Develop on the Spot.'

The other at a police station.

****

'Prawn cocktail, steak and Black Forest gateau with all the trimmings,' squeaked Goldie Bouncer in her poshest voice.

'The same for me, and make it snappy,' said Sid, winking at Goldie.

The Head Waiter bowed and hid the look of dislike on his face. Who did they think they were trying to fool? 'Of course, sir,' he murmured.

Sid lifted a glass bubbling with the best champagne. Goldie picked up her glass and twisted her arm through his.

What a team they made!

'To us,' said Sid.

'To us,' replied Goldie.

Then as if pulled by some strange force they both looked in the same direction.

The Rigid-Smythes and the Wolfbanes were walking together into the dining room!

Goldie sprayed her dainty sip of champagne all over the place. Sid's hand stayed frozen in midair. Goldie's eyes swivelled sideways to where the two families were settling themselves down around a big table.

'Sid,' hissed Goldie. 'I don't know what's going on and I don't want to know. But they ain't seen us yet and we've got to get out of here fast.'

Sid's eyes snapped open twice but he still couldn't move.

'Sid!' hissed Goldie again.

'Shuddup. I'm thinking.'

Behind them a pair of French doors led onto a patio.

'We'll go through these doors and round the side of the hotel,' Sid muttered. 'Then you pack and meet me in the lobby. I'll get the briefcase out of the safe.'

'Two prawn cocktails, sir?'

A waiter held out two crystal goblets filled to the top with prawns in pink sauce.

'We've changed our minds,' said Sid, rudely.

But he didn't notice that the waiter wasn't at all surprised.

Chapter Twelve

Pearl Wolfbane thought back to the morning when she had first seen Ruby out of her window. It seemed ages ago and yet it was no time at all. Who would have thought so much could have happened? Ruby was the best friend she had ever had. Across the table she watched Simon and Clod laughing. She had never seen Clod so happy. As for Simon, he didn't even look the same!

Now here they all were sitting in the fanciest hotel in town around a beautiful table sparkling with silver and crystal. Of course Pearl knew that something serious was going on. Sid Bouncer was a bad man and any minute now, the police were going to arrest him. But that wasn't the whole reason they were all dressed up and going out together. Pearl knew it was to celebrate the friendship between the two families.

Ruby leaned over and nudged Pearl in the ribs. Her eyes sparkled like black pearls.

'Who would have thought it?' she whispered with a huge grin on her face.

And Pearl knew exactly what she was talking about.

Across the table Pamela and Anaconda were laughing and talking.

'You must tell me where you do your shopping,' said Anaconda. 'It's Pearl's birthday soon and I'd love to get it right, if you see what I mean.'

'I know exactly what you mean,' replied Pamela. 'I've got it wrong myself for so long!'

Clod and Simon were studying the menu upside down. They had a bet on that Simon's parents would notice before anyone else.

'Bet they don't,' said Clod. 'They're too busy talking and besides they don't seem to care about those things any more.'

'Bet they do,' said Simon. 'Some things will never change.'

They agreed to give it five minutes.

Five minutes later, Clod won the bet. A bubble of glee rose up in Simon's chest and he burst out laughing. Maybe he didn't know his parents that well after all.

'Any minute now,' said Boris, looking at his watch.

Dudley swallowed nervously and nodded. The sergeant at the police station had been very interested in the photograph and what Dudley had to say when the Wolfbanes and the Rigid-Smythes called in on their way to the Regency Ritz. Apparently, the police had been following the careers of Sid and Goldie Bouncer for a number of years. The problem, explained the sergeant, was that they had never been able to get enough evidence to put them in jail. Dudley had been flabbergasted. 'You mean Sid's done this sort of thing before?'

'Goodness me, yes!' replied the sergeant. 'You'd be surprised how many people fall for it.'

The sergeant shook his head. 'It's exactly the same scam every time. The only things that ever change are Sid's name and the colour of Goldie's hair.'

So the police sergeant, Dudley and Boris worked out a plan that would trap Sid and Goldie red-handed but not in any way spoil the children's fun and everyone else's evening out.

Because it wasn't just Pearl who knew that this was an extra-special occasion. Both the Wolfbanes and the Rigid-Smythes were delighted with their new friends. So all that Dudley had to do was identify his briefcase in the hotel safe and the moment Sid tried to collect it, he and Goldie would be arrested.

'But how will we know when they're gone?' Dudley had asked nervously.

The policeman had laughed. 'We'll send you in a big bottle of champagne.'

'Excellent,' said Boris smiling.

****

Dudley looked at his watch again. It was only a minute since he had checked it but the seconds felt like hours.

'Compliments of the hotel.'

A waiter put an enormous silver bucket on the table. Inside it was an even bigger bottle of champagne!

It was the moment Dudley had been waiting for!

Sid and Goldie Bouncer would not be cheating anybody else again for a long, long time!

Across the table, Pearl and Ruby saw their parents exchange the most extraordinary looks. Both girls could sense a huge feeling of relief and a huge happiness. Even though they knew nothing of what Sid and Goldie had been planning, they knew something very important had happened and that things were going to be different for them all from now on.

There was a huge POP! as the waiter opened the champagne and quickly filled everyone's glass. 'I would like to propose a toast,' said Boris Wolfbane.

He stood up and smiled around the table. 'To friends and neighbours!'

Dudley Rigid Smythe went bright red then he stood up beside Boris.

'To friends and neighbours,' he cried.

And even though it was the fanciest hotel in town and somewhere people always mind their manners, Anaconda and Pamela, Ruby and Pearl and Clod and Simon all jumped up and let out the loudest cheer they could manage.

As Pearl shouted at the top of her voice, she suddenly thought of *Felicity – A Happy Girl's Story* and the perfect world that it described.

In that moment, Pearl realized that it didn't matter if people lived different lives. It didn't matter if Anaconda and Boris had a mud hole or if the Rigid-Smythes had a sparkling blue swimming pool.

Pearl and Ruby turned to each other at the same time. It was as if they were both thinking the same thing.

While the others were laughing and cheering,

Pearl and Ruby wrapped their arms around each other and hugged as hard as they could.

'You're my best friend,' muttered Ruby fiercely.

'You're my best friend, too,' whispered Pearl. She pulled back and wiped away the tears that were shining in her eyes.